THE WORLD OF
NORM

MAY NEED FILLING IN

ORCHARD BOOKS
338 Euston Road, London NW1 3BH
Orchard Books Australia
Level 17/207 Kent Street, Sydney, NSW 2000

First published in 2014 by Orchard Books

A Paperback Original

ISBN 978 1 40833 427 0

Text © Jonathan Meres 2014
Illustrations © Donough O'Malley 2014

A CIP catalogue record for this book is available from the British Library.

1 3 5 7 9 10 8 6 4 2

Printed and bound by CPI Group (UK) Ltd, Croydon, CR0 4YY

Orchard Books is a division of Hachette Children's Books,
an Hachette UK company.

www.hachette.co.uk

JONATHAN MERES

THE WORLD OF
NORM
MAY NEED FILLING IN

ORCHARD

Welcome to the World of Norm!

Norm

Brian

Dave

Mum and Dad

THROB THROB

John
the dog

Grandpa

Chelsea

Mikey

Norm's Vital Statistics

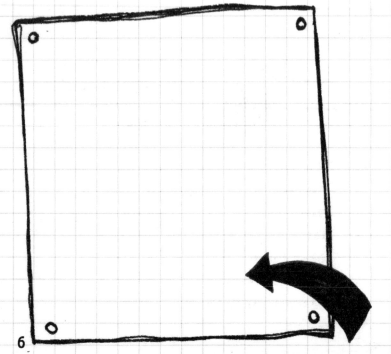

Age: Nearly 13
Height: 1.53 metres
Eyes: Two
Likes: Bikes
Doesn't like: Chelsea
Favourite word: Abso-flipping-lutely
Least favourite word: Hormones
Thinks: Everything's unfair

6

Draw a picture of Norm here:

My Vital Statistics

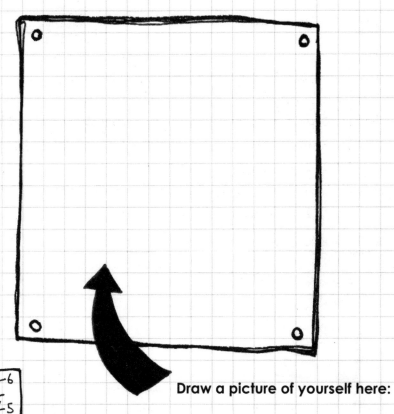

Draw a picture of yourself here:

Age:

Height:

Eyes:

Likes:

Doesn't like:

Favourite word:

Least favourite word:

Thinks:

7

Even More About Me:

Favourite colour:

Tastiest food:

Worst food:

Favourite drink:

Best ever movie/
TV show:

Most hated movie/
TV show:

Best school subject:

Best day of the week:

Favourite sport:

Most hated household chore:

Best holiday/day out:

Best song of all time:

Worst song of all time:

Worst thing you've ever heard anyone say about you:

Nicest thing you've ever heard anyone say about you:

Most annoying thing in the whole wide world:

9

Norm Wants to Know...
So tell the truth.

Are you scared of going to the dentist or doctor?

Have you ever managed to get away with doing
something really bad?

What would you do if an alien landed in your
back garden?

Have you ever promised to keep a
friend's secret and then told someone else?

Do you use deodorant every day?

- -

Have you ever searched the house for your Christmas presents before Christmas?

- -

- -

What's the worst advice you've ever been given?

- -

- -

What's the latest you've ever been for school?

- -

- -

Complete the Picture

'Aw, Man!'

Being forced to visit his perfect cousins at the weekend makes Norm go:

List the most boring chores you have to do:

tidy room

- ---
- ---
- ---
- ---
- ---
- ---
- ---
- ---

Norm's Life is <u>So</u> Unfair because...

- Mikey gets a brand new iPad

- His little brothers always get their own way

- He's not World Mountain Biking Champion (yet...)

- He can't afford to pimp up his bike

- Grown-ups don't have to go to school

- He's not allowed to eat pizza every day

- Perfect cousin Danny keeps showing off his bang-up-to-date smartphone

- Even the dog gets more attention than he does...

My Life is <u>So</u> Unfair because...

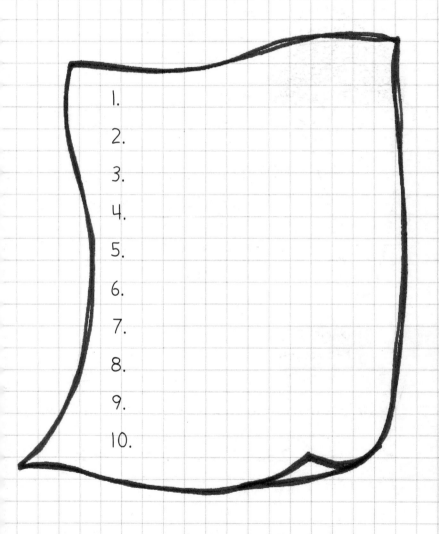

1.

2.

3.

4.

5.

6.

7.

8.

9.

10.

Picture Crossword

Here are some things that Norm likes having in his life.
Can you write their names in the crossword grid?
Go to page 186 for the answers.

TIP: Count the
letters in each
word first.

Just Flipping Say It

Fill in the bubbles with questions, statements or anything else you feel like saying.

Spot the Difference

Take a look at these two pictures of Norm's family on a typical car journey.
Can you find nine differences between them?

Go to page 186 for the answers.

The Doodle Brothers

Brian and Dave are just SO ANNOYING! Help Norm get his own back on his little brothers by doodling on them.

How about adding a moustache, sideburns or a beard? A ludicrous hairstyle? Maybe a silly hat or some earrings?

Brian and Dave's Really Stupid Jokes

What do you get if you cross a centipede and a parrot?
A walkie talkie.

Ha Ha

What did the cookie say when it fell over?
'Crumbs!'

There were two fish in a tank. One of them said 'Do you know how to drive this thing?'

How does a monkey make toast?
Under the gorilla.

HA HA

What's brown and sticky?
A stick.

What gets wetter, the more it dries?
A towel.

Why did the banana go to the sick room?
It wasn't peeling very well.

What did the scarf say to the hat?
'You go on ahead and I'll hang around.'

Where do baby apes sleep?
Apricots.

How do you know if there's an elephant in your bed?
Because you need a ladder to get into it.

What do you call a deer with no eye?
No idea!

My Stupid Joke

Are Norm's family 'normal'?

Norm doesn't think so. Why can't he have nice, normal parents like Mikey's? Life can be so un-flipping-fair! How normal are Norm's family compared with yours?

Look at the descriptions below and give each of Norm's relatives a score on a scale from 1 – 10 (1 being absolutely normal, 10 being ABSO-FLIPPING-LUTELY barking!). Then turn the page and do the same for your family.

GRANDPA

Obsessed by his allotment. Tries to 'pump up' his shed by painting it mint green. Buys an iPad but can't work out how to use it. Talks about ancient pop groups that Norm's never heard of.

Score ☐

MUM

Always glued to TV shopping channels. Buys smaller spoons to help her lose weight. Enjoys going to Ikea on a regular basis. Demands that Norm make her cups of coffee – when he's not even in the house.

Score ☐

DAD

Gets fired from his job but keeps it secret from Norm's mum. Becomes highly stressed very easily. Has strange throbbing vein on side of head. Is obsessed with saving money and keeps turning off the lights.

Score ☐

DAVE

A smart cookie for his age. A tough negotiator when it comes to money. But he still believes Norm when he tells Dave that Santa Claus is really a woman.

Score ☐

BRIAN

Plays 'hilarious' pranks, such as taking out the batteries from Norm's alarm clock to make him late. A secret bedwetter. Loves *Lord of the Rings*.

Score ☐

My Family

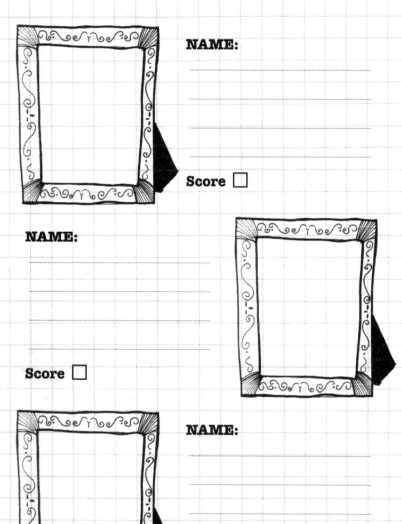

NAME:

....

....

....

Score ☐

NAME:

....

....

....

Score ☐

NAME:

....

....

....

Score ☐

NAME:

Score ☐

NAME:

Score ☐

NAME:

Score ☐

29

What keeps you awake at night?

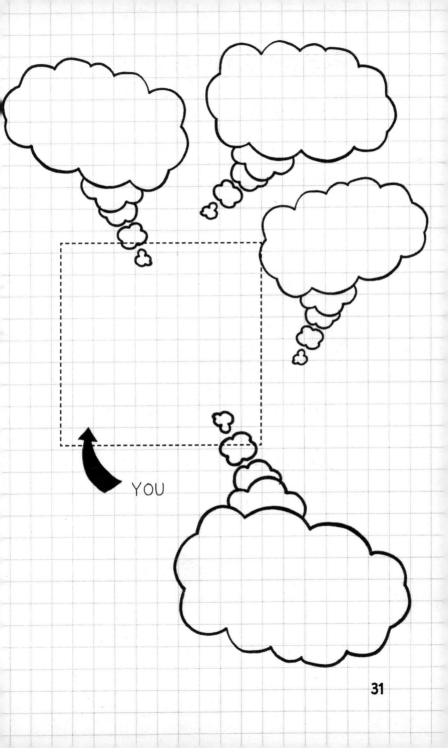

The Many Faces
of Norm

Norm experiences a lot of different emotions in his rollercoaster of a life. One minute he's deliriously happy (like when he was finally bought an iPad), the next he's disappointed (the iPad was pink).

SURPRISED

ANGRY

Can you imagine Norm's different expressions as he goes through a 'Norm-al' day? Can you draw them? Give it a try!

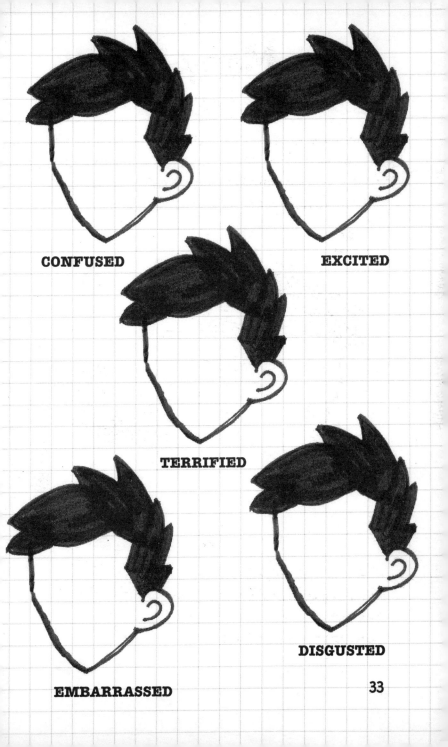

CONFUSED

EXCITED

TERRIFIED

EMBARRASSED

DISGUSTED

33

You're an Animal!

If you could be any animal in the world, what would you be – and why?

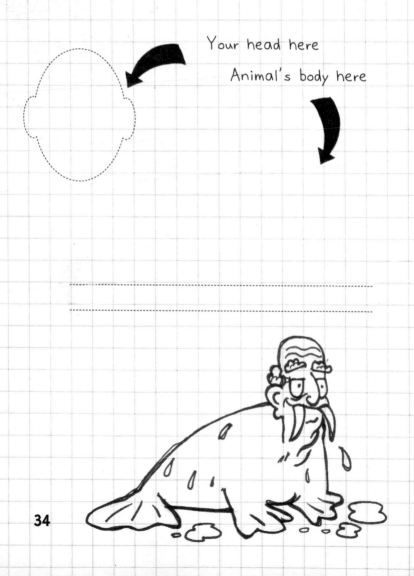

Your head here

Animal's body here

Your head here

Animal's body here

Norm's List of Unlikely Things to Happen

- He becomes Prime Minister

- Dave or Brian commit a random act of kindness

- Grandpa gets into hip-hop

- Mum and Dad give him £100 for being such a great son

- He and Chelsea become great friends

My List of Unlikely Things to Happen

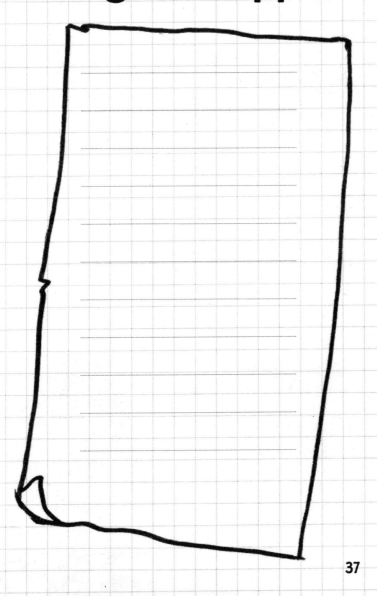

Norm's Name Wordsearch

Can you find the names of Norm's family, friends and other people he knows in this wordsearch? They might be up, down, across or diagonal.

Alan	Dave	Becky
Chelsea	John	Zak
Linda	Brian	Alice
Mikey	Danny	Ed

All right, **NORMAN?**

J	O	N	S	V	M	C	K	B	O	M	Z
K	H	A	Z	A	B	P	A	L	A	N	P
C	M	I	K	D	H	E	G	C	D	H	F
E	A	R	C	T	S	U	Y	L	M	O	C
V	H	B	F	L	P	K	U	Y	T	J	Y
A	L	I	E	B	C	I	N	O	V	E	B
Y	P	H	Z	E	C	I	L	A	U	D	K
E	C	A	B	O	D	C	S	U	A	T	N
M	A	K	A	Z	K	L	I	N	D	A	C
J	C	S	V	B	Y	A	N	J	L	M	J
O	Z	M	I	K	E	Y	I	N	G	D	H
I	L	A	N	Z	M	O	D	A	V	E	Y

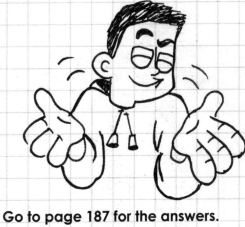

Go to page 187 for the answers.

39

It's a Dog's Life!

John is the family dog.

Norm is the family's eldest son.

Does John the dog have an easier life than Norm? Think about it:

• Dogs don't have to do any homework or boring chores around the house.

• If a dog lets off a bottom burp he's not expected to apologise or leave the room. He just looks surprised.

• Dogs get forgiven if they pee next to the fridge.

• They get stroked and called 'cute'.

• Dogs are allowed to run around the park madly, making lots of noise.

• If a dog doesn't want to hear something, he can pretend not to understand.

Name that Dog

It's not always easy to name a dog. Brian and Dave suggested...

Simon Cowell

Jesus

Limahl
(singer in a 1980s pop group.)

Norm suggested Microwave – or Buttcheek...

BUTTCHEEK

Eventually, 'John' was chosen – after Grandpa's favourite member of the Beatles, John Lennon.

Name Your Dog

If you had a dog, what would you name it? Give each of these very different dogs a suitable name:

Write dog's name here

43

John's Wooftastic Word Grid

How much do you know about dogs? Solve the clues going across to find something that dogs enjoy in the vertical box. Go to page 187 for the answers.

1. The sound a dog (or an annoying little brother) makes when it's not very happy.

2. What a dog wags when it's happy.

3. When you go for a walk, your dog takes the _____.

4. Another sound a dog makes – also something you find on a tree.

5. Dogs have a great sense of:

a) humour b) urgency c) smell

1.
2.
3.
4.
5.

Mad Dog Jokes

How do you stop a dog from smelling?
Put a peg on his nose.

How do you know when a dog's really stupid?
He chases parked cars.

Scratch Scratch

What should you do if a dog chews up your pencil?
Use a pen instead.

What is a dog's favourite food?
Anything that's on your plate.

Why can't dogs dance?
Because they have two left feet.

Why are dogs like big trees?
They both have a lot of bark.

Why do dogs run in circles?
Because they can't run in squares.

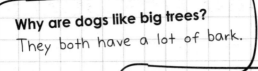

How do you know when a dog's got bad breath?
His bark is worse than his bite!

Where should smelly dogs go on holiday?
Hong Pong.

My dog joke:

That's My Dog!

Draw your ideal dog.

Different Dogs

There are all kinds of dogs in the world.
Can you fill in the missing letters to complete
these dog breeds? Go to page 188 for the answers.

Sp_n_el   Bo_er

Te_ _ier   _eagle

La_ _ador   _ achshund

_oodle

Norm's family dog,
John, is a

cock-a-_ _ _.

Clue — the missing word is also
the name of something smelly
that you wouldn't want to slip in.

Freaky Futures

When Norm's grandpa was young, the world was very different. Could he ever have predicted iPads and smartphones, pizza and pot noodles?

Write your five predictions for when you're as old as Grandpa:

1.

2.

3.

4.

5.

Grandpa's Mixed Greens

Norm always knows where to find Grandpa – on the allotment, tending his prized vegetables.

But it's all gone a bit pear-shaped for Grandpa today. He's dropped his latest crop and they're all mixed up. Can you unscramble the letters to find the vegetables? Go to page 188 for the answers.

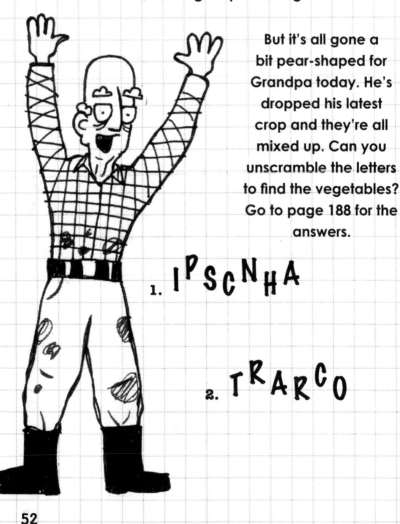

1. IPSCNHA

2. TRARCO

3. CORBLCIO

4. AOPTOT

5. NEAB

1. _ _ _ _ _ _ _ _

2. _ _ _ _ _ _ _

3. _ _ _ _ _ _ _ _ _

4. _ _ _ _ _ _ _

5. _ _ _ _

Jokes from Grandpa's Allotment

Which vegetable do you not want to find on a boat?

A leek.

Which is the fastest vegetable of all?

The runner bean.

Which is the laziest vegetable?

The couch potato.

What's green and likes camping?

A Brussels Scout.

How do you start a vegetable race?

'Veggie, steady, go!'

Why are radishes so clever?

Because they're well red.

What did the tomato plant say?

Nothing — it just let out a little vine.

What did the rabbit say to the carrot?
'It's been nice gnawing you.'

What's the difference between pea soup and roast beef?
Anyone can roast beef.

What happens when two peas fight?
You get black-eyed peas.

What do you call an over-sized Halloween vegetable?
A plumpkin.

What's small and red, and whispers?
A hoarse radish.

What's invisible and smells of carrots?
A rabbit's fart.

55

WHIZZ

My veggie joke:

Would You Rather?

You HAVE to choose
one option...

Share your bed with a farting dog? ☐

Share your bed with a little brother
who pees in his sleep? ☐

Go to Ikea ☐

Go to school ☐

WOOF!

Eat a plate of cold tofu ☐

Eat a plate of cold cauliflower cheese ☐

Have a babysitter who's a zombie ☐

Have a babysitter who's a vampire ☐

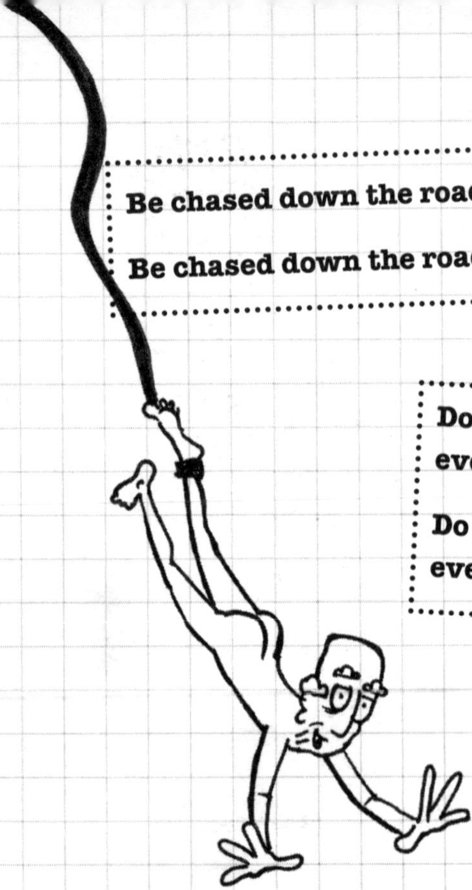

Be chased down the road by the school bully ☐

Be chased down the road by a Velociraptor ☐

Do a paper round every day ☐

Do the washing up every day ☐

Climb Mount Kilimanjaro ☐

Bungee jump off a high bridge ☐

Mount Kajagoogoo

Fall off your bike onto your arm ☐

Fall off a horse onto your bum ☐

Find yourself naked in a cinema ☐

Find yourself naked in a supermarket ☐

Eat a toothpaste sandwich ☐

Eat a raw onion ☐

Passable Pyjamas

Dinosaur pyjamas are not a good look for Norm. Design him some new ones that won't make him blush.

Dreams Can Be Weird

NORM'S WEIRD DREAM:

I'm naked in a supermarket and everyone is looking at me!

MY WEIRD DREAM:

Perfect Put-downs

Some people can be so

annoying!
Memorise these put-downs
and you'll never again be
lost for words with your
nosy neighbour or
sarky sibling:

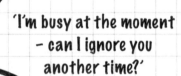

'I'm busy at the moment
– can I ignore you
another time?'

'I thought about you
all day today. I was at
the zoo.'

'I can tell you're lying –
your lips are moving.'

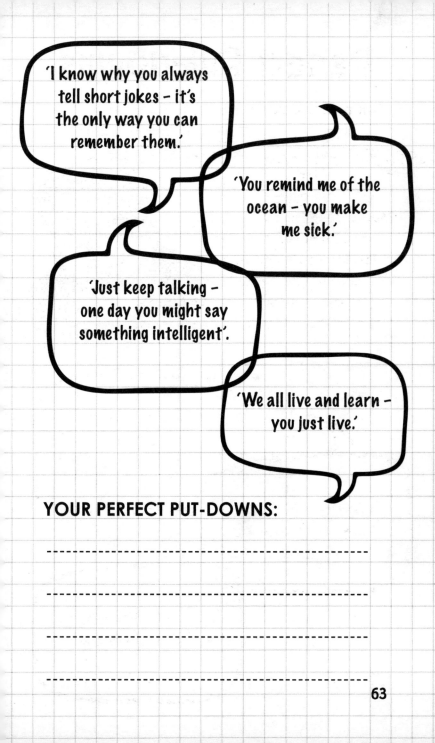

'I know why you always tell short jokes – it's the only way you can remember them.'

'You remind me of the ocean – you make me sick.'

'Just keep talking – one day you might say something intelligent'.

'We all live and learn – you just live.'

YOUR PERFECT PUT-DOWNS:

63

Odd One Out

Look carefully at these pictures of Norm, Norm's dad and Mikey. One picture in each group is not the same as the others. Can you find it?

1. NORM

A)

B)

C)

D)

2. NORM'S DAD

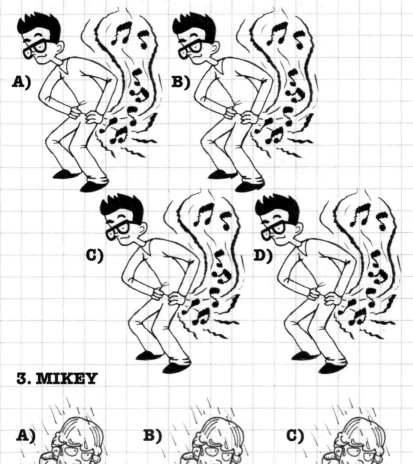

3. MIKEY

Go to page 188 for the answers.

You've Got a Friend

Norm and Mikey have been best mates for as long as they can remember. They first met when they were both in nappies, so they know a lot about each other.

How would you describe your friend? Circle the words that you think best suit him or her.

Random

Cool

Smelly

Musical

Weird

Energetic

Grumpy

Chatty

MY MATE'S NAME:

Funny   Brilliant

            Shy

Friendly   Sporty

            Clumsy

Thoughtful

                    Sarcastic

        Helpful

Confident   Hyper

            Kind

Clever   Imaginative

        Lazy

                Quiet

Human

Mikey's Mistakes

Mikey often sends Norm instant messages. Only trouble is, his spelling and punctuation are even worse than Norm's – and that's flipping saying something! Can you correct Mikey's spelling mistakes? Go to page 188 for the answers.

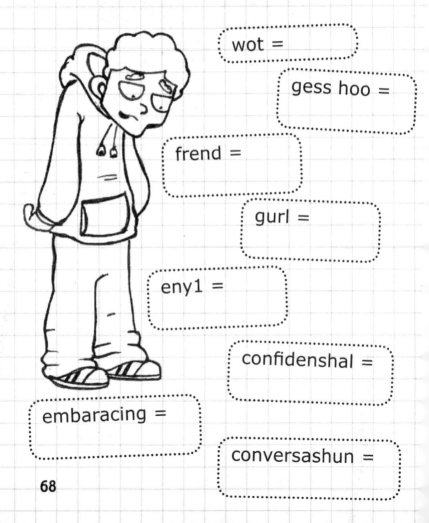

wot =

gess hoo =

frend =

gurl =

eny1 =

confidenshal =

embaracing =

conversashun =

gud =

alredy =

thort =

Wordz I Have Trubble Spelling...

Accurate Acronyms

Mikey does odd jobs for his dad – but secretly thinks
he's the CEO of his dad's company
(Chief Executive Officer).

WHAT DO THESE ACRONYMS MEAN?

BTW

FYI

IMO

LOL

VIP

TMI

BRB

IRL

GAL

AFK

CTN

ASAP

Go to page 188 for the answers.

MY MOST OVER-USED ACRONYM IS :

Annoying Things Parents Say

Add your parents' words of wisdom...

- You'd better pull your socks up or else.

- Cheer up, it's not the end of the world.

- It's happening whether you like it or not.

- Do you think I'm stupid? (Probably best not to answer that one!)

- You left the computer/TV/lights on – again.

- I can read you like a book.

- How much longer are you going to be in there? (toilet)

-

-

-

-

-

Dish the Dirt on Your Parents

Do your parents ever let you get away with stuff that they shouldn't?

_____

Were your parents cool when they were young?

Yes ☐ No ☐

Draw the funniest outfit or hairstyle you've seen on one of your parents in an old photo.

How strict are your parents on a scale of 1 (pushovers) to 10 (super-strict)?

_____

THROB THROB

Is it easy to distract them, and how?

_____

_____

_____

_____

unbe-FLIPPING-lievable

What's the biggest secret you've kept from your parents? (You'd better hide this book if you want to keep it a secret!)

_____

_____

_____

_____

Have you ever spotted your mum or dad doing something they shouldn't?

_____

_____

_____

_____

What's the stupidest thing one of your parents has ever done?

_____

_____

_____

_____

Get Shirty

Design a T-shirt to suit a member of your family.

Norm's dad's
T-shirt

I'M
STRESSED!

THIS T-SHIRT IS FOR:

When Parents Just Don't Listen...

Things you could say to check if your mum and dad are really listening to you...

- I'm not really your son/daughter.

- I was raised by zebras in the Belgian rainforest.

- A bunch of aliens in a spaceship just landed in the garden.

- My people await me. Farewell, my so-called mother/father!

-

-

-

-

-

Bonjour

Money, Money, Money...

DAD'S MONEY SAVING IDEAS

1. Switch off lights, computer, TV – everything – to save electricity.

2. Buy cheap value food from the supermarket – like own-brand coco pops.

3. Save water by only flushing toilets if absolutely necessary. (i.e. if someone's done something very smelly)

4. Close all doors to keep the heat in.

5. Don't buy any expensive gadgets for the kids.

NORM'S MONEY SAVING IDEAS

1. Buy less food for Brian and Dave – they're only little, after all.

2. Always buy the BOGOFs at the supermarket (especially the Jammie Dodgers).

3. Sell John the dog – but would anyone pay good money for a stinky cock-a-poo?

4. Ban Mum from watching any TV shopping channels. Ever.

5. Sell Brian and Dave's toys and use the money to get an iPad for Norm.

MY MONEY SAVING IDEAS

1. ....
2. ....
3. ....
4. ....
5. ....
6. ....
7. ....
8. ....
9. ....
10. ....

Dot-to-Dot

What animal has the bully Ryan O'Toole been turned into?

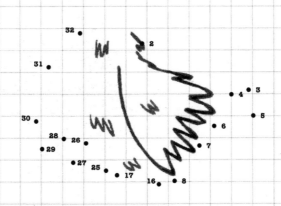

Are you a Norm Nerd?

Think you're a Norm fan? But how much do you really know about Norm, his friends and his family? Test your knowledge to rate your 'Norm nerdness' factor. Or just take a guess.

1. Mikey is embarrassed to admit to Norm that he's got...

a. ...hormones ☐

b. ...nits ☐

c. ...girls' pants on ☐

2. What is little brother Dave's favourite movie?

a. Mary Poppins ☐

b. The Wizard of Oz ☐

c. Dumbo ☐

3. What language does John the dog understand?

a. French ☐

b. Chinese ☐

c. Polish ☐

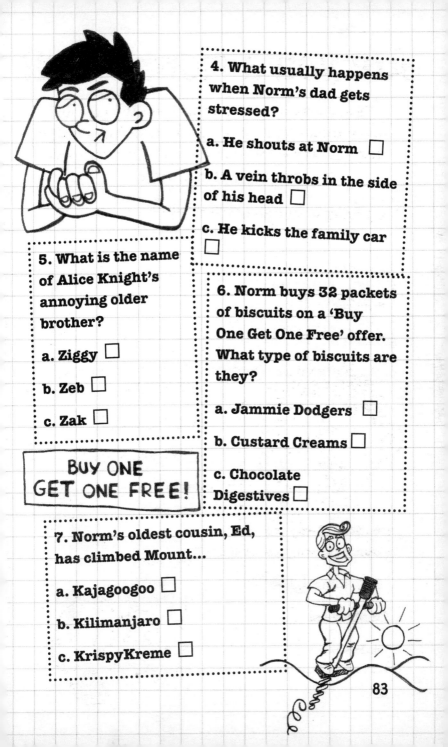

4. What usually happens when Norm's dad gets stressed?

a. He shouts at Norm ☐

b. A vein throbs in the side of his head ☐

c. He kicks the family car ☐

5. What is the name of Alice Knight's annoying older brother?

a. Ziggy ☐

b. Zeb ☐

c. Zak ☐

BUY ONE GET ONE FREE!

6. Norm buys 32 packets of biscuits on a 'Buy One Get One Free' offer. What type of biscuits are they?

a. Jammie Dodgers ☐

b. Custard Creams ☐

c. Chocolate Digestives ☐

7. Norm's oldest cousin, Ed, has climbed Mount...

a. Kajagoogoo ☐

b. Kilimanjaro ☐

c. KrispyKreme ☐

83

8. What do Norm, Dave and Brian usually have for breakfast?

a. Own brand rice krispies ☐

b. Own brand sugar puffs ☐

c. Own brand coco pops ☐

9. When Norm finally gets an iPad, what colour is it?

a. Lilac ☐

b. Pink ☐

c. Red ☐

10. When Chelsea offers to help Norm with his paper round, what does she do with the newspapers?

a. Dumps them behind a hedge ☐

b. Burns them on a bonfire ☐

c. Takes them home to read ☐

11. At the primary school nativity play, Norm played the part of Joseph. What part did jealous Zak Knight get?

a. Goat ☐

b. Donkey ☐

c. Sheep ☐

12. Which one of the following things does John the dog do?

a. He drinks out of the toilet ☐

b. He sits on the toilet to do a poo ☐

c. He flushes the toilet with his nose ☐

Now mark your scores.
Go to page 188 for the answers.
How many questions did you get right?

9-12: Notable Norm Nerd

Impressive! You're a massive fan of Norm and you don't care who knows it. Bet you've all got all the 'World of Norm' books arranged in number order on your bookshelf. Keep up the good work!

5-8: Nearly Norm Nerd

Hmmm, not bad. You've maybe not read all the 'World of Norm' books yet but you're getting there. Keep on going and you'll soon attain Notable Norm Nerd status.

4 or less: Not even slightly a Norm Nerd

Oh dear! Have you even read a 'World of Norm' book lately? We suggest you get hold of a copy of the latest book and take it with you everywhere – even the loo. Only then will your Nerd status rise. Start soon – there's an e-norm-ous amount to catch up on!

Norm Wants to Know...
So tell the truth.

How many jokes can you tell off the top of your head?

_____

_____

Have you ever heard a weird noise in the night and had to sleep with the light on afterwards?

_____

_____

How would you liven up a dull party?

_____

_____

Do you know the difference
between a 'desert' and a 'dessert'?

_____

_____

Can you write your name with the hand you don't usually write with?

- -

What do you always take with you when you go out?

- -

- -

Which TV or film character is most like you?

- -

- -

What's your dream job?

- -

- -

Multi-tasking Norm

Sitting on the toilet, eating pizza and checking Facebook, all at the same time, isn't easy – but practice makes perfect.

PIZZA

MULTI-TASKING ME

What can you do at the same time?

Invent a Gadget

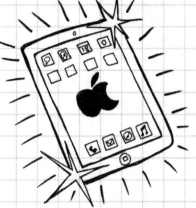

Norm loves computers, iPads and smartphones. What great new gadget would you like to see in the shops?

The Stupid Things We Do

The most stupid thing I've ever done was...

....

....

....

....

....

The most stupid thing my friend has ever done was...

....

....

....

....

....

I rode my bike really fast up a ramp and crashed into the garage...

Create a Magazine

Norm's fave magazine

My ideal magazine

Bike-U-Like Jokes

Why can't a bike stand up on its own?
Because it's two-tyred
(too tired, geddit?)

What's the hardest thing about learning to ride a bike?
The pavement.

When is a bike not a bike?
When it turns into an alleyway.

Why are all bicycles haunted?
Because they have spooks in them!

First Farmer: What shall I buy — a new cow or a bicycle?

Second Farmer: You'd look pretty stupid riding a cow.

First Farmer: I'd look even more stupid trying to milk a bicycle.

What's so great about riding a bike?
It's 'wheely' fun.

Norm (on phone): Is this the local bike shop?

Bike shop owner: That depends on where you live.

My bike joke:

Brilliant Bike Wordsearch

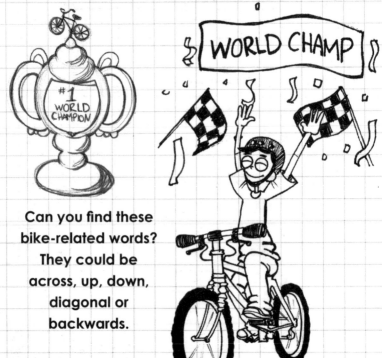

Can you find these bike-related words? They could be across, up, down, diagonal or backwards.

Wheel   Pedal   Helmet
Brake   Chain   Suspension
Spoke   Saddle   Fork
               Handlebars

J	O	N	H	E	L	M	E	T	O	M	Z
K	H	A	Z	A	F	P	L	E	E	H	W
L	A	D	E	P	H	O	G	C	D	H	F
E	N	R	C	T	S	U	R	L	M	O	C
V	D	B	F	L	P	K	U	K	T	H	Y
A	L	I	E	B	C	E	N	O	A	E	B
Y	E	H	Z	E	L	I	L	I	U	D	R
E	B	A	B	D	D	C	N	U	A	E	A
M	A	K	D	Z	K	L	I	N	D	K	K
J	R	A	V	B	Y	A	N	J	L	O	E
O	S	M	I	R	E	Y	I	N	G	P	H
I	N	O	I	S	N	E	P	S	U	S	Y

Go to page 189 for the answers.

Get on Your Bike

Norm's design for a bike challenge:

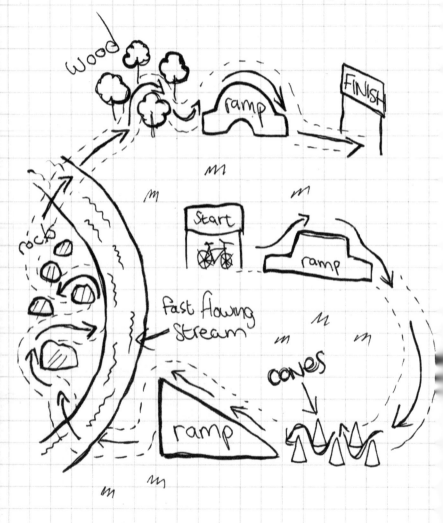

Your ideas for a bike challenge:

Pimp That Bike

Make this bike fit for a future World Mountain
Biking Champion.

Norm's ideas

- eye-catching front forks

- attach a radio or a state-of-the-art speaker system

- adapt the seat to a high back

    - paint on a great design

- give it a name

    - add one outstanding feature — like wings — to really get you noticed

Dot-to-Dot

While the cat's away, Norm will play – with the
pizza he's found under his bed!
Join the dots to find out which creature
Norm has turned into.

Norm's Niggles

THINGS THAT REALLY GET ON NORM'S NERVES...

1. Chelsea, the annoying girl next door. Who posted a photo of Norm – naked – on Facebook (even though he was just a baby at the time).

2. Homework – is it only Norm that's noticed 'studying' has the word 'dying' in it?

3. Tofu – like eating pieces of dry, foamy bath sponge.

4. Walks. Long, healthy, boring walks. Completely pointless.

5. Norm's 'perfect' cousins. Not only do they get brilliant school reports, they enjoy healthy walks and eating tofu. Enough said.

6. Annoying little brothers – especially when they hog the computer or burst into the toilet interrupting your magazine reading.

THINGS THAT REALLY GET ON YOUR NERVES...

1. ....

2. ....

3. ....

4. ....

5. ....

The Numbers Game

**Fill in the spaces with whatever you think are the
right numbers. (There are no wrong answers.)**

Amount of pocket
money you should
get every week
£____

A good time to get up
on a weekend morning
_____:_____

A reasonable bedtime
____:____

How long you should spend brushing your
teeth at night
Hours _____ Minutes _____

Amount of money the tooth fairy used to leave under your pillow £____

How long a typical school day should be
Hours _____ Minutes _____

The amount of money you'd like to fall out of your next birthday card £____

How long you should be able to spend in the toilet without being shouted at
Hours _____
Minutes _____

How much money you should give for your teacher's Christmas present
£____

One Day...

Circle your choices and fill in the gaps.

One day I'll be a **World Mountain Biking Champion/ doctor/world-class athlete/bus driver/ genius scientist/ teacher.**

I'll live in a terrace/country house/ stylish apartment with its own swimming pool/fishing lake/football pitch/games room/jacuzzi/cinema room.

In my spare time I'll go jetskiiing/scuba diving/quad biking/skinny dipping.

I'll visit places like New York/Barbados/ Paris and _____ , travelling in my own personalised plane/tour bus/limousine.

I'll most likely be a billionaire/ millionaire/squillionaire and I'll run a company called _____ which makes _____ .

I will meet the Prime Minister/President of the United States/_____ .

I will be the first person to land on Mars/discover a cure for all known diseases/save the planet from a zombie invasion/_____ .

Because I'm so generous I will use lots of my money to help _____ .

Signed_____ .

Marvellous Menus

Norm's Dream Meal:

Starter:
Unlimited garlic bread and dips

Main:
18-inch deep crust pepperoni pizza from Wikipizza with extra cheese. Hot potato wedges and ketchup on the side. Definitely no salad!

Dessert:
Four scoops of mint choc-chip ice cream topped with lashings of spray-on cream and multi-coloured sprinkles.

100% TOP NOTCH

Ken & Terry's
ICE CREAM
COMPANY

MINT
CHOC
CHIP

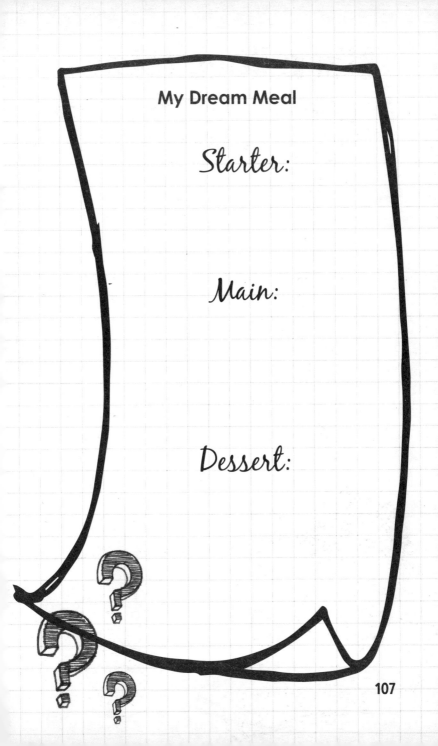

My Dream Meal

Starter:

Main:

Dessert:

Top Toppings

Everyone has a favourite pizza. Can you complete these tasty pizza toppings just by filling in the vowels? (That's a, e, i, o or u.)

Ch _ _ s _

H _ m

M _ shr _ _ m

T _ m _ t _

_ l _ v _

P _ pp _ r _ n _

Ch _ ck _ n

P _ n _ _ ppl _

P _ pp _ r

S _ _ s _ g _

Answers on page 189.

Create an Ice Cream

100% TOP NOTCH

Ken&Terry's
ICE CREAM
COMPANY
MINT
CHOC
CHIP

Norm's fave ice cream

My new flavour

Top Five Best Foods

1. _ _ _ _ _ _ _ _ _ _ _ _ _ _ _ _ _ _ _

2. _ _ _ _ _ _ _ _ _ _ _ _ _ _ _ _ _ _ _

3. _ _ _ _ _ _ _ _ _ _ _ _ _ _ _ _ _ _ _

4. _ _ _ _ _ _ _ _ _ _ _ _ _ _ _ _ _ _ _

5. _ _ _ _ _ _ _ _ _ _ _ _ _ _ _ _ _ _ _

Top Five Worst Foods

1. _____
2. _____
3. _____
4. _____
5. _____

Tasty Word Grid

Is your idea of a balanced diet holding
a pizza in each hand?
Complete this gastronomic word quiz and you'll find
a very important pizza ingredient in the vertical box.
Go to page 190 for the answers.

1. They're not saucercakes or mugcakes,
they're _____.

2. Mikey's mum makes the best hot
_____ in the world. Mmmm!

3. They come in a tin and are easy to
heat up and eat on toast.

4. Adults seem to drink a lot of
tea and _____.

5. You usually get loads of these when Trick
or Treating at Halloween. They're delicious
but bad for your teeth.

6. In Norm's opinion, chips without
this on top are just...pointless.

1.
2.
3.
4.
5.
6.

113

Jokes from Pizza World

Which is the left side of a pizza?
The side that hasn't been eaten.

'Waiter, will my pizza be long?'
'No sir, it will be round.'

Which type of pizza do dogs like?
Puparoni.

What was Good King Wenceslas's favourite pizza?
Deep pan, crisp and even.

What does Dr Who have with his pizza?
Dalek bread.

Why aren't there more jokes about pizza?
Because they're way too cheesy!

My food joke:

Biscuit Brainteasers

Norm's been sent to the supermarket with a ten-pound note to buy biscuits. Can you help him? Go to page 190 for the answers.

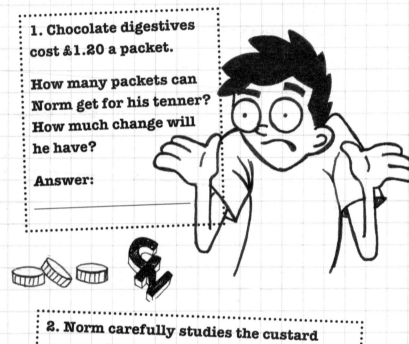

1. Chocolate digestives cost £1.20 a packet.

How many packets can Norm get for his tenner? How much change will he have?

Answer:
_____

2. Norm carefully studies the custard creams. He works out he could get 22 packets for his money, with 10p change. How much does each packet of custard creams cost?

Answer: _____

3. Jammie Dodgers are on a BOGOF offer (that's not rude, by the way – it means Buy One Get One Free).

They normally cost 62p a packet. How many packets can Norm get? And how much change will he have?

Answer _____

Which biscuits do you think Norm should buy and why?

_____

_____

What's your fave biscuit and how many can you usually eat?

_____

_____

Bedroom Bedlam

Does your bedroom look anything like Norm's?

Scratch

Take a long look at Norm's messy bedroom. Now cover up the picture with a piece of paper and see how good your memory is. Can you write down ten objects that are lying on his bedroom floor? Give yourself one minute and see how you do.

1. ....

2. ....

3. ....

4. ....

5. ....

6. ....

7. ....

8. ....

9. ....

10. ....

It's All French to Me

Read these sentences that Norm's written for his French homework and match them to the correct meaning.
Bonne chance!

1. Je m'appelle Norm. ☐

2. J'ai presque treize ans. ☐

3. Mikey est un beignet confiture. ☐

4. Je n'ai pas d'argent. ☐

5. Ma vie, c'est injuste. ☐

a. I don't have any money.

b. I'm nearly thirteen.

c. My life is unfair.

d. Mikey is a jam doughnut.

e. My name is Norm.

Go to page 190 for the answers.

Write about yourself and your friends. In French.

Je m'appelle _____

Ma vie, c'est _____

_____

_____

_____

_____

Je m'appelle...?

Classroom Jokes

Why do the French class always need the toilet?
Because they're always going 'Oui, oui'.

Teacher: What's the capital of France?
Norm: Er, 'F'?

Why is an English lesson like being in prison?
Because you know you're in for a long sentence.

What's the history teacher's favourite fruit?
Dates.

Teacher: Spell the word 'weather'.

Mikey: W-E-V-A-R.

Teacher: That's the worst spell of weather we've ever had.

Which suntan lotion do maths teachers use?

The one with the highest factor.

What do the history class and school dinners have in common?

Ancient Grease.

Teacher: Name the four food groups.

Norm: Er, fast, junk, frozen and tinned.

My classroom joke:

Confession Time
Spill the beans.

Do you somehow know if a person is looking at you – even if you can't see him/her? (Spooky...)

Have you ever cheated in a board game?

What would be your ideal holiday?

Have you ever eaten food that's past its sell-by date?

Which school subject would you immediately ban if you had the power?

Do you know all the words to 'Rudolph the Red-Nosed Reindeer'? (Prove it.)

Can you blow up a balloon with your nose?

If you became invisible, what is the first thing you would do?

Bright Ideas that Might Just Work...

- An 'off' switch for annoying people

- Self-tying shoelaces

- Smartphones that beam themselves back to their owners when called

- Dogs that clear up their own mess

- Make Friday into Funday so that every weekend is three days long

- Electronic gadgets that can be charged up by blowing into them

- Smaller spoons for people who are trying to eat less (suggestion from Norm's mum)

- Make it illegal for girls named after football teams to live next door?

- Self-cleaning teeth?

  - Mute button for little brothers and sisters

-
-
-
-
-
-

Confession Time

Have you ever told a big fat lie?
A porky pie?
Norm has – on a few occasions –
but only when he really had to.

Confess your 'porky' here:

Rate Your Embarrassment

Life can be really embarrassing sometimes. Like, if someone posts a photo of you stark naked on Facebook. That's a full-on five-star blush. Or if you accidentally call your teacher 'Mum' in front of the whole class. (More like a four-star.)

Write down your embarrassing experiences and rate them:

BLUSH RATING

*   **A little bit warm in the facial area**

**   **A light pinkness of the cheeks**

***   **You're hot and flushed as if you've been running a mile a minute**

****   **You look like a tomato**

*****   **Your face is now the colour of a baboon's backside**

What Happened:

_____
_____
_____
_____
_____
_____
_____

RATING:

What Happened:

_____

_____

_____

_____

_____

_____

_____

RATING:

House Rules Rule!

1. Don't use the computer when I want to use it.

2. Don't pee in my bed (that includes little brothers!).

3. Don't follow me around the house asking stupid questions.

4. Don't bother me when I am sitting peacefully on the toilet reading a magazine.

5. Don't nag me about homework or tidying my bedroom.

6. Don't ask me to walk the flipping dog.

7. Do ask me if I need snacks, drinks or pocket money.

MY HOUSE RULES:

1.

2.

3.

4.

5.

6.

7.

Create a Superhero

ZAK'S SUPERHERO

(based on Norm, unfortunately)

Name: Cauliflower Boy
Special superpower: Producing wind

MY SUPERHERO

Name:
Special superpower:

Rate that Smell

Some smells are really nice. But not all smells... Put these smells in order according to how nice/ horrible you think they are, Number 1 being the nicest, Number 10 being the worst.

1. ....

2. ....

3. ....

4. ....

5. ....

6. ....

7. ....

8. ....

9. ....

10. ....

137

Sleepover Wishlist

When Zak Knight invites Mikey for a sleepover, he promises the following:

· A ninety-
six-inch flat-
screen HD TV

· A wide selection of completely
inappropriate Xbox games

· They will be allowed to go
to bed at literally any time
they want

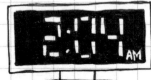

MY SLEEPOVER WISHLIST

Accidents Will Happen...

Norm once slipped in a puddle of sick and sprained his wrist. Ouch!

Describe the worst injury you've ever had and how it happened:

_____

_____

How many times have you been to hospital?

_____

Have you ever had a plaster cast?

_____

Did people write stuff on it? And if so, what?

_____

Show the locations of any past wounds, injuries or scars here:

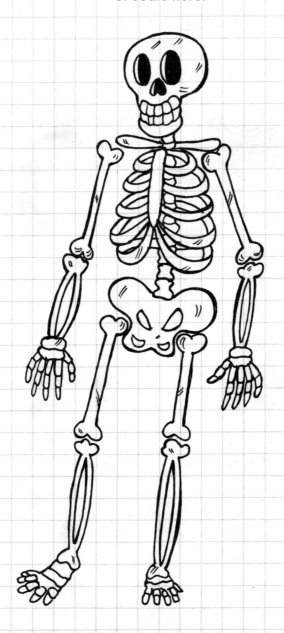

Odd One Out

Look carefully at these pictures of Norm, Norm's mum and Dave. One picture in each group is not the same as the others. Can you find it?

1. NORM

A)

B)

C)

D)

2. NORM'S MUM

3. DAVE

Go to page 190 for the answers.

Spot the Difference

Take a look at these two pictures of Norm, Grandpa and John the dog. Can you find eight differences between them? Go to page 191 for the answers.

A)

B)

Shopping Mad Wordsearch

Norm's mum and dad have been to IKEA – again. Can you find all the items they've bought in this wordsearch? Answers are on page 191.

P	D	N	S	V	E	S	A	V	O	M	Z
S	H	A	Z	A	B	P	L	L	A	N	S
L	A	M	P	D	H	E	W	C	D	N	A
E	A	R	C	T	S	H	O	L	I	O	U
V	H	B	F	L	I	K	B	A	T	J	C
A	L	I	E	S	C	I	T	O	V	E	E
R	P	H	K	E	C	R	L	A	U	D	P
E	C	A	B	O	U	C	S	U	A	T	A
D	A	K	A	C	H	A	I	R	D	A	N
D	C	S	V	B	Y	A	N	J	L	M	S
A	Z	M	U	K	I	Y	I	N	G	D	H
L	B	T	N	Z	M	O	X	A	R	E	Y

147

Nine Items or Less

Mikey's been to the supermarket for some essential items. What has he put in his basket? Unscramble the words to find out. Go to page 192 for the answers.

L E R C A E

_ _ _ _ _ _

U E I C J

_ _ _ _ _

S T B I C S U I

_ _ _ _ _ _ _

SGRIFNEISHF

_ _ _ _   _ _ _ _ _

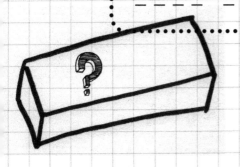

THIS
AISLE
NINE
ITEMS
OR
LESS

149

SEPA

_ _ _ _

KMLI

_ _ _ _

EORDAONDT

_ _ _ _ _ _ _ _

Dot-to-Dot

Join the dots to find out which creature Norm wishes he could change into...

Clue: If Norm was this creature, he could blend in nicely with his surroundings.

Things which are completely POINTLESS

NORM'S POINTLESS THINGS:

Poetry

Simultaneous equations

Smelly dogs

Going for long walks

Salad

Chips without ketchup on them

NOW FOR YOURS:

POINTLESS FOOD

....
....
....
....
....
....
....

POINTLESS ACTIVITIES

....
....
....
....
....
....
....

POINTLESS SCHOOL SUBJECTS

....

....

....

....

....

....

....

....

....

ENGLISH

MATHS

FRENCH

HISTORY

154

POINTLESS PEOPLE

....
....
....
....
....
....
....

Weird Body Behaviour

Have you personally experienced any of the following?

Brain freeze (after eating ice-cream)

Yes ☐ No ☐

Twitching eye

Yes ☐ No ☐

Random itching

Yes ☐ No ☐

Long bouts of hiccups

Yes ☐ No ☐

Sneezing fits

Yes ☐ No ☐

Smelly feet

Yes ☐ No ☐

Loud uncontrollable burp

Yes ☐ No ☐

Rumbling stomach

Yes ☐ No ☐

Clicking knee or other bones

Yes ☐ No ☐

Restless legs

Yes ☐ No ☐

Windy bottom

Yes ☐ No ☐

PARP

Rumbling stomach

Yes ☐ No ☐

Uncontrollable laughter – when you shouldn't be laughing

Yes ☐ No ☐

Runny nose

Yes ☐ No ☐

Bleeurrgh!

NORM'S GUT-CHURNING EXPERIENCES

- Stepping into dog poo first thing in the morning (bare feet — not good)

- Slipping bum first into a pool of warm vomit

- Being licked by the dog when it's just been drinking from the toilet

- Spending time with his 'perfect' cousins

- Being forced to eat tofu

YOUR 'BLEEURRGH!'
EXPERIENCES...

-
-
-
-
-

Great Achievements of Our Time

What Norm's perfect cousins (Danny, Becky and Ed) have achieved between them...

Directed Shakespeare's Hamlet

Played piano at the old folk's home

Practised Capoeira (a Brazilian art form/ martial art)

Climbed Mount Kilimanjaro

My Great
(or not so great)
Achievements...

Tricky True or False

Here are some fascinating 'facts' you might have noticed in the World of Norm stories. But do you know if they're true or false?
Write T or F in the box – and have a guess if you're not sure. The answers are on page 192.

1. BOGOF means Buy One Get One Free. ☐

2. A cock-a-poo is a dog that's a cross between a cocker spaniel and a poodle. ☐

3. Cock-a-poo flu is a real illness that dogs get. ☐

4. It is illegal to snog a goat. ☐

5. There's no such language as Belgian. ☐

6. Belgium has a rainforest and zebras live there. ☐

CACKLE CACKLE CACKLE CACKLE

7. Money doesn't grow on trees. ☐

8. Kajagoogoo were a pop group famous in the mid-eighties. ☐

Crossword Challenge

Test your Norm knowledge with these
challenging clues, then go to page 192
for the answers.

ACROSS

1. Name of Norm's extremely irritating girl
   neighbour. Also the name of a football team.

2. Norm's maths teacher, Mrs Simpson, has a
   nickname. What is it?

3. What Norm's mum likes doing in her spare time.

4. Mikey's favourite deodorant.

DOWN

5. This stinky pet is named after a famous member
   of the Beatles.

6. Mikey's got these racing around his body. Which
   is why he might suddenly be interested in girls
   and needs to use quite a lot of Clue Number 4.

7. The stinky pet in Number 5 has really bad
   _ _ _ _ _ _. Phew!

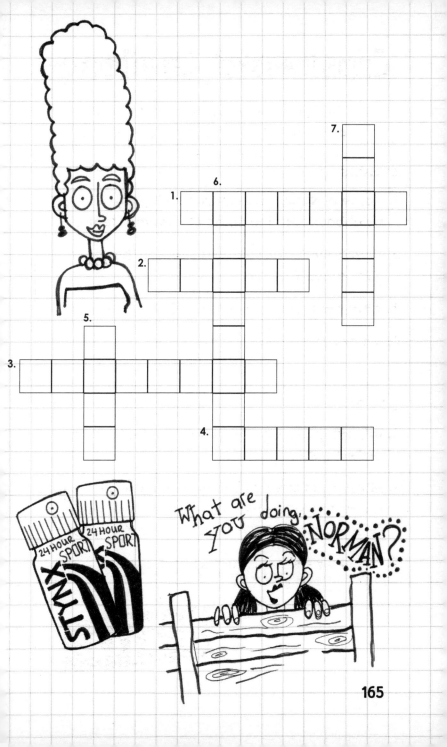

165

Norm Wants to Know...
So tell the truth.

What's the worst comment you've ever had on a school report?

What's the most annoying thing a member of your family does?

What single thing would make your life much better?

Have you ever dozed off during a boring event?

166

Have you ever taken part in a talent show?

How much would you pay to take a day off school?

Have you ever faked an illness to get out of doing something you didn't want to do?

What's the greediest you've ever been?

Chelsea wants to know...

Norm's unbe-flipping-lievably annoying neighbour has turned up again...

Are you a geek? Yes ☐ No ☐

Are you as stupid as you look?
Yes ☐ No ☐

Why are you wearing what you're wearing?

Are you trying to hide something?

What's in your pockets?

Can I video you and put it on YouTube?

Now get Chelsea back by asking her some annoying questions:

The Stupidest Jokes I Know

My unbe-FLIPPING-lievable Day

A comic strip by

....

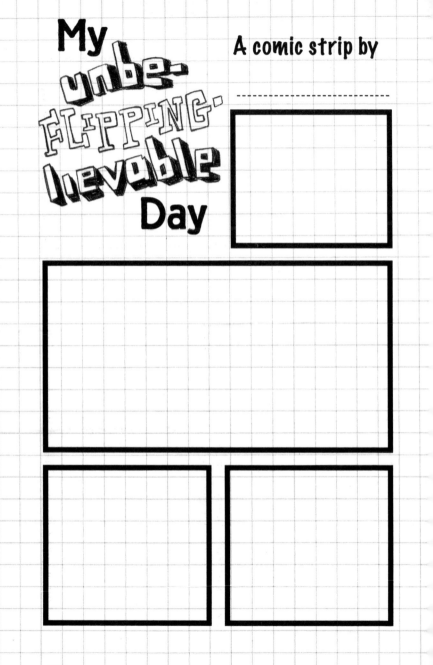

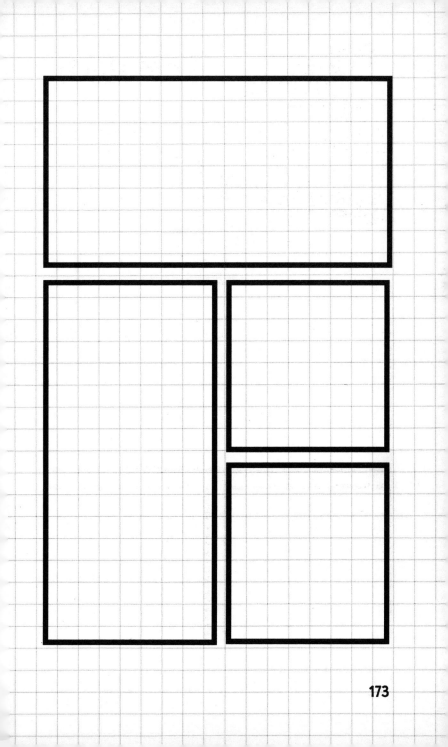

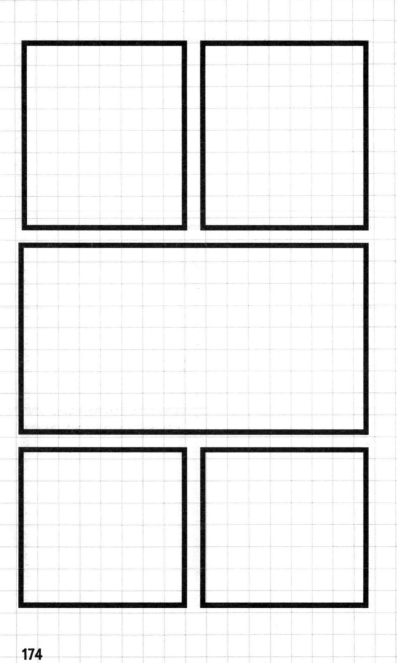

174

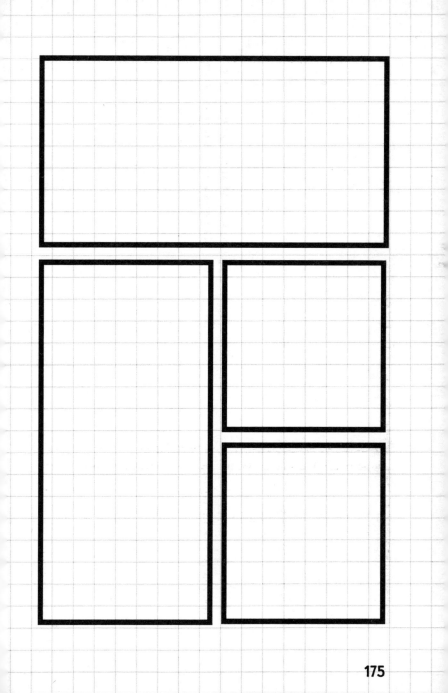

Things to do before you get to Grandpa's age

Norm's grandpa is really quite old. Before you get to his age do you think you will have done any or all of these things? Tick if you have already.

- Sleep under the stars for a night
  Done it ☐ **Not yet** ☐

- Jump into a freezing cold swimming pool
  Done it ☐ **Not yet** ☐

- Try a food that you thought you didn't like, and realise that you do like it after all
  Done it ☐ **Not yet** ☐

- Say 'Hello' in three languages
  Done it ☐ **Not yet** ☐

- Learn how to moonwalk
  Done it ☐ **Not yet** ☐

- Wear a furry animal onesie out in public
  Done it ☐ **Not yet** ☐

- Find your way somewhere using a compass
  Done it ☐ **Not yet** ☐

- Take part in a flashmob
  Done it ☐ **Not yet** ☐

- Eat dessert before dinner
  Done it ☐ **Not yet** ☐

- Put a clip on YouTube and get at least 1,000 hits
  Done it ☐ **Not yet** ☐

- Eat wild blackberries you've just picked from a bush
  Done it ☐ **Not yet** ☐

- Go on the scariest ride at a theme park
  Done it ☐ **Not yet** ☐

- Sledge down a snowy hill
  Done it ☐ **Not yet** ☐

- Be the first on the dance floor at a party
  Done it ☐ **Not yet** ☐

- Learn an impressive magic trick and perform it
  Done it ☐ **Not yet** ☐

- Change your hairstyle completely
  Done it ☐ **Not yet** ☐

- Bake a loaf of bread – and eat it
  Done it ☐ **Not yet** ☐

- Write a song
  Done it ☐ **Not yet** ☐

- Take a 'selfie' with someone famous
  Done it ☐ **Not yet** ☐

Norm's Family
Fun Quiz

Which person or pet in Norm's family is most like you?
Tick the boxes.

The first thing you notice when you wake up in the morning is that...

a. You're totally naked in the middle of a supermarket. Phew – it's only a dream. ☐

b. Your bed's wet – again. ☐

c. You're still alive! ☐

d. The house is really messy and everyone needs to tidy their rooms. ☐

e. You've done a messy poo next to someone's bed. ☐

Whoopee! You are given an iPad for a birthday present. What's the first thing you do with it?

a. Get straight onto YouTube to watch a selection of mountain biking videos. ☐

b. Get straight onto the Lord of the Rings fan site. ☐

c. Fiddle with the iPad for hours trying to work out how it turns on. Then give up and go off to do some gardening. ☐

d. Spend the day doing online shopping. ☐

e. Chew it into tiny little pieces. ☐

Your idea of a really fun afternoon is...

a. Pimping up your bike and building a ramp to ride on. ☐

b. Taking the dog for a walk in the park. ☐

c. Going down the allotment to put some manure on your courgettes. ☐

d. Taking a trip to IKEA and forcing your family to go with you. ☐

e. Running around in circles, while doing SBDs (Silent But Deadlies). ☐

Your favourite food is...

a. Any Wikipizza pizza ☐

b. Mum's cauliflower cheese ☐

c. Anything that doesn't give you wind or get under your false teeth. ☐

d. Anything that you don't have to cook. ☐

e. Anything you can chew on while rooting around the bins. ☐

What's your ambition in life?

a. To become World Mountain Biking Champion. ☐

b. To eat up all your greens and be allowed a pudding afterwards. ☐

c. To grow a massive prize-winning marrow. ☐

d. To win a £10,000 shopping spree in your local department store. ☐

e. To drink from the toilet whenever you feel like it.. ☐

What really upsets you?

a. The unfairness of life. ☐

b. Bullying. ☐

c. Frost ruining your tomatoes. ☐

d. Your online shopping deliveries not arriving on time ☐

e. Being put on a lead. ☐

What sound do you make when you're approaching someone from behind?

a. The whizzing sound of mountain bike wheels, followed by the screech of brakes. ☐

b. The creak of the creaky floorboard behind the computer, as you creep up on whoever's online. ☐

c. A slight panting and shuffling – you're not as young as you used to be. ☐

d. The rustling sound of your carrier bags, groaning with shopping. ☐

e. A loud panting and slurping noise, topped off by a full-blown smelly fart... ☐

CREAK!

What would make your life much better?

a. Tons of gadgets, including a top-of-the-range smartphone and an iPad in the colour of your choice. ☐

b. If your older sibling was nicer to you, and let you go on the computer more often. ☐

c. If you had a brand-new painted wooden shed with a cosy armchair inside it. ☐

d. If you could lie on the sofa all day, drinking coffee and watching TV shopping channels. ☐

e. If the whole world was a giant park in which you could poo as much as you wanted. ☐

What is one of the worst things you've ever done?

a. Secretly kept money that wasn't yours. ☐

b. Took out the batteries from your brother's alarm clock so that he was late for school. ☐

c. You think you did something really naughty when you were at school but it was so long ago, you can't remember anything about it. ☐

d. Spent vast amounts of money on things that you will never use, like extra-small spoons. ☐

e. Eaten an out-of-date pizza and thrown up on the bathroom floor. ☐

It's most embarrassing when...

a. You accidentally call your teacher 'Mum' in front of the whole class. ☐

b. Your dog runs away from you and you have to chase him round the park, shouting. ☐

c. Your shed looks shabby compared to all the others on the allotment. ☐

d. Your massive credit card bills arrive every month. ☐

e. You never get embarrassed, not even when you let off random farts in public places. ☐

RESULTS

Count your answers to see if you got mostly As, Bs, Cs, Ds or Es. Then see who you're most like!

> Mostly As
> You are most like Norm

You really don't ask for much in life. A decent mountain bike, regular pocket money, a few state-of-the-art gadgets and the occasional pizza are all you really need. But somehow, things never seem to work out for you. Life is just so unfair...

Mostly Bs
You are most like Brian

You're a simple soul who loves being with animals and playing fantasy games, whenever you get the chance to go on the computer. You have a naughty streak though and often get away with your pranks. But if something upsets you, admit it – you can be a bit of a crybaby.

Mostly Cs
You are most like Grandpa

You're never happier than when you're hanging out at the allotment, tending your vegetables. You are wise, patient and helpful, always ready to welcome anyone into your shed who needs advice. There isn't much you don't know about – you've seen it all!

Mostly Ds
You are most like Norm's mum

There's nothing you enjoy more than lounging around on the sofa, browsing through the TV shopping channels and drinking endless cups of coffee. 'Shop till you Drop' is your motto. But sometimes you wonder why you've got so many boxes of stuff you don't need, cluttering up your hall...

Mostly Es
You are most like John the dog

Energetic and fun-loving, you scamper through life without a care in the world, letting off stinky farts whenever you fancy. Personal hygiene may not be your best point but you are extremely loving and affectionate – even if your breath does stink of rancid toilet water...

185

Answers

Pages 16-17

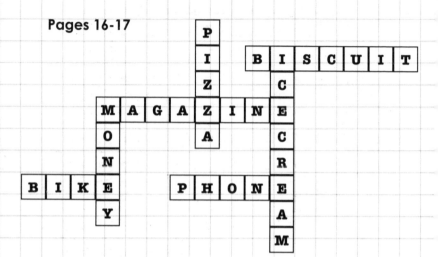

Pages 20-21

J	O	N	S	V	M	C	K	B	O	M	Z
K	H	A	Z	A	B	P	A	L	A	N	P
C	M	I	K	D	H	E	G	C	D	H	F
E	A	R	C	T	S	U	Y	L	M	O	C
V	H	B	F	L	P	A	U	Y	T	J	Y
A	L	I	E	B	C	I	N	O	V	E	B
Y	P	H	Z	E	G	I	L	A	U	D	K
E	C	A	B	O	D	C	S	U	A	T	N
M	A	K	A	Z	K	L	I	N	D	A	C
J	C	S	V	B	Y	A	N	J	L	M	J
O	Z	M	I	K	E	Y	I	N	G	D	H
I	L	A	N	Z	M	O	D	A	V	E	Y

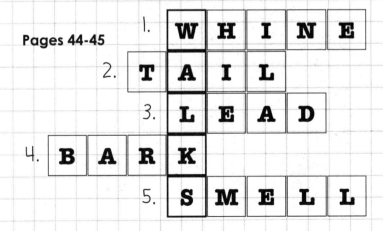

1. | W | H | I | N | E |

2. | T | A | I | L |

3. | L | E | A | D |

4. | B | A | R | K |

5. | S | M | E | L | L |

187

Page 50

Spaniel
Terrier
Labrador
Poodle
Boxer
Beagle
Dachshund
Cock-a-poo

Pages 52-53

1. Spinach
2. Carrot
3. Broccoli
4. Potato
5. Bean

Pages 64-65

1. C)
2. B)
3. C)

Pages 68-69

what, guess who, friend, girl, anyone, confidential, embarrassing, conversation, good, already, thought

Pages 70-71

By The Way, For Your Information, In My Opinion, Laugh Out Loud, Very Important Person, Too Much Information, Be Right Back, In Real Life, Get A Life, Away From Keyboard, Can't Talk Now, As Soon As Possible

Pages 82-85

1. A) 2. B) 3. C) 4. B) 5. C) 6. A) 7. B) 8. C) 9. B) 10. A) 11. C) 12. A)

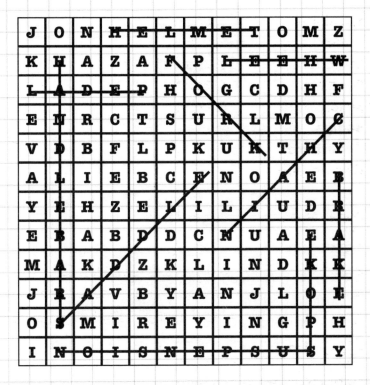

J	O	N	H	E	L	M	E	T	O	M	Z
K	H	A	Z	A	P	P	L	E	E	H	W
L	A	D	E	P	H	O	G	C	D	H	F
E	N	R	C	T	S	U	R	L	M	O	C
V	D	B	F	L	P	K	U	K	T	H	Y
A	L	I	E	B	C	F	N	O	A	E	B
Y	E	H	Z	E	L	I	L	I	U	D	R
E	B	A	B	D	D	C	N	U	A	E	A
M	A	K	D	Z	K	L	I	N	D	K	K
J	R	A	V	B	Y	A	N	J	L	O	E
O	S	M	I	R	E	Y	I	N	G	P	H
I	N	O	I	S	N	E	P	S	U	S	Y

Page 108

Cheese, ham, mushroom, tomato, pepperoni, olive, chicken, pineapple, pepper, sausage

Pages 112-113

1.	C	U	P	C	A	K	E	S

2.	C	H	O	C	O	L	A	T	E

3.	B	E	A	N	S

4.	C	O	F	F	E	E

5.	S	W	E	E	T	S

6.	K	E	T	C	H	U	P

Pages 116-117

1. 8 packets (with 40p change).

2. Custard creams are 45p a packet.

3. He can get 32 packets of Jammie Dodgers with 8p change. Normally he could get 16 packets at 62p (altogether £9.92) but as they're on offer he gets double the packets.

Pages 120-121

1. E) 2. B) 3. D) 4. A) 5. C)

Pages 142-143

1. B)
2. D)
3. A)

190

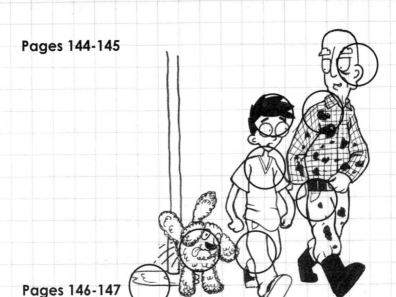

P	D	N	S	V	E	S	A	V	O	M	Z
S	H	A	Z	A	B	P	L	L	A	N	S
L	A	M	P	D	H	E	W	C	D	N	A
E	A	R	C	T	S	H	O	L	I	O	U
V	H	B	F	L	I	K	B	A	T	J	C
A	L	I	E	S	C	I	T	O	V	E	H
R	P	H	K	E	C	R	L	A	U	D	P
E	C	A	B	O	U	C	S	U	A	T	A
D	A	K	A	C	H	A	I	R	D	A	N
D	C	S	V	B	Y	A	N	J	L	M	S
A	Z	M	U	K	I	Y	I	N	G	D	H
L	B	T	N	Z	M	O	X	A	R	E	Y

Pages 148-150

Cereal, Juice, Biscuits, Fish fingers, Peas, Milk, Deodorant

Pages 162-163

1. T, 2. T, 3. F (Norm made it up), 4. F (no laws about goats as far as we know), 5. T (the three official languages of Belgium are Dutch – aka Flemish – French and German.) 6. F, 7. T (according to Norm's dad), 8. T (ask your parents if you don't believe it).

Pages 164-165

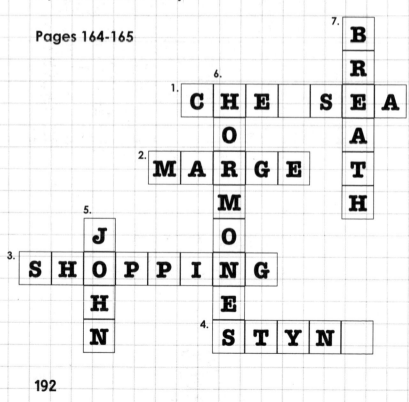

"Hilarious stuff from one of my comic heroes!"
Harry Hill

Want more Norm? Don't miss

THE WORLD OF NORM

MAY NEED REBOOTING

OUT NOW!
Read on for a sneak peek...

ORCHARD BOOKS
www.orchardbooks.co.uk

CHAPTER 1

Norm knew it was going to be one of those days
when he woke up and found himself in the middle
of The French Revolution.

"Norman?" said a strangely familiar-sounding
voice.

Uh? thought
Norm groggily.
What was
going on?

Had he fallen asleep in front of the telly? And if so, where was the flipping remote control? Because there **had** to be something better on than **this!**

"You haven't been **asleep**, have you?" said the voice.

There was a burst of laughter. Norm looked around to see a sea of grinning faces looking back at him. Suddenly he knew **exactly** what was going on. He **had** fallen asleep. But **not** in front of the telly. He'd fallen asleep in **class!** No flipping wonder the voice had sounded strangely familiar. It was the voice of his history teacher, Miss Rogers!

"Late night, was it, Norman?"

"What?" yawned Norm.

"Pardon," said Miss Rogers.

"What?" said Norm.

"**Pardon!**" said Miss Rogers. "Not **what!**"

"Oh, right. Sorry," said Norm.

"Late night, was it?"

"Erm, yeah, kind of," said Norm.

"Good," said Miss Rogers. "Pleased to hear it."

Norm was getting more confused by the second. And he'd been pretty confused in the **first** place. "What? I mean, pardon?"

"Well I'd hate to think you'd dropped off because of my **teaching**."

"No, no, course not, Miss Rogers," said Norm quickly.

There was more laughter. As it happened though, the night before had been a late night – most of which Norm had spent Googling around for

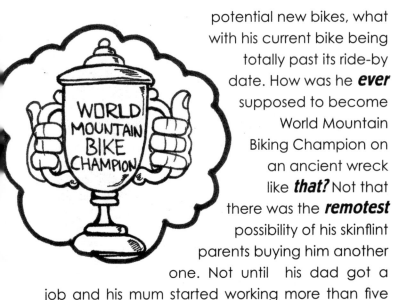

potential new bikes, what with his current bike being totally past its ride-by date. How was he ***ever*** supposed to become World Mountain Biking Champion on an ancient wreck like ***that?*** Not that there was the ***remotest*** possibility of his skinflint parents buying him another one. Not until his dad got a job and his mum started working more than five minutes a week at the flipping cake shop there wasn't, anyway. And even then they'd probably want to blow all their money on flipping food and clothes and electricity and stuff, claiming that that was somehow more ***important.*** It was ***so*** unfair.

"What were you doing?" said Miss Rogers.

Norm shrugged. "Just thinking."

"I meant what were you doing last night?" said Miss Rogers. "Or don't I want to know?"

Norm thought for a moment. How did **he** know whether his teacher wanted to know what he'd been doing last night or not? What was he? Psychic or something?

"Well, Norman?"

"Looking at bikes," muttered Norm.

"Geek," laughed a voice from the back.

Norm turned around to see Connor Wright, the captain of the football team, smirking at him.

"What was that?" said Norm.

"Er, nothing," said Connor Wright.

"There's nothing geeky about looking at bikes!" spat Norm.

"Whatever," said Connor Wright.

"Better than flipping **football**," muttered Norm.

"You reckon?"

"Yeah, I do actually," said Norm.

"Just 'cos you're rubbish at football," sniggered Connor Wright.

"I'm not rubbish," said Norm. "I'm really good."

"Oh yeah?"

"Yeah," said Norm. "I just don't play, that's all."

"That's quite enough, you two," said Miss Rogers.

Norm sighed. He knew that Connor Wright was right. He really *was* rubbish at football. But Connor Wright wasn't *completely* right. The real reason Norm chose not to play football was that Norm hated football more than just about anything. Well, apart from going for walks. And living in a stupid little house with paper-thin walls and only one toilet. And most vegetables. But apart from that, Norm hated football more than just about anything.

"Open your homework diary please."

Diary? thought Norm. Not **diaries?** He must have misheard. He glanced around the rest of the class. But no one else had made a move.

"Well, Norman?" said Miss Rogers.

Norm pulled a face. "Just me?"

Miss Rogers nodded. "Just you."

"But..."

"I don't see anyone **else** asleep, do you?"

"Give them a few more minutes," mumbled Norm under his breath.

"Oh, dear. That's unfortunate," said Miss Rogers.

"What is?" said Norm.

"Well, that's just doubled the size of your punishment exercise."

Norm heard the words, but it was several seconds before he fully comprehended what they actually meant.

"Punishment exercise?"

"Well, of course," said Miss Rogers. "What do you expect?"

Norm opened his mouth to say something – but suddenly thought better of it and closed it again. Miss Rogers clearly wasn't going to change her mind now. Things weren't about to get any better. They could only get worse. Same as flipping usual.

CHAPTER 2

"You fell **asleep?**" said Mikey in utter disbelief.

"Yes, I fell asleep, Mikey," said Norm.

"You actually fell **asleep?**"

Norm sighed. "Yes, Mikey. I actually fell asleep."

"In **history?**" said Mikey as if that was somehow worse than falling asleep in maths, or geography.

"Yes, Mikey," said Norm, beginning to get more and more exasperated. "In history."

"Whoa," said Mikey.

Gordon flipping Bennet, thought Norm. The way Mikey was going on anybody would think he'd got changed into his flipping pyjamas first – not just accidentally nodded off for a few seconds.

"I didn't **mean** to, Mikey!"

"Well I should hope not," said Mikey.

Norm looked at his best friend. "Have you never fallen asleep, then?"

Mikey looked puzzled. "In school, you mean?"

Norm sighed again. "No, I mean have you ever just generally fallen asleep?"

"What?"

"Of **course** I mean in flipping school, you doughnut!"

"Oh, right," said Mikey. "Erm, no, I don't think so."

Course not, thought Norm. Silly question really. Mikey would **never** do a thing like that, would he? He'd be too busy sticking his hand up and getting every single question right! Just like he used to in primary school. Of course it wasn't Mikey's fault that he was just that little bit better at everything than Norm was. Norm knew that. It was still flipping annoying though. The only consolation, as far as Norm was concerned, was that he and Mikey weren't actually in the same class very often now that they were in secondary school. They were in different classes for nearly all subjects. In fact some days the only time they actually saw each other was at lunch when they walked round the playing field together, chatting. Which was exactly what they were doing now.

"How come?" said Mikey eventually.

"How come what?" said Norm.

"You fell asleep."

Norm looked at Mikey again. For someone who

was supposed to be reasonably intelligent, he didn't half ask some stupid questions sometimes.

"How come I fell *asleep?*"

Mikey nodded.

"Because I was *tired*, Mikey!" said Norm. "Why else do you think I fell asleep?"

"Well, obviously you were *tired*, Norm," said Mikey. "What I meant was *why?*"

"Why was I tired?"

"Yeah."

"Because I didn't go to bed till really late last night."

"Yes, but *why?*" persisted Mikey.

Gordon flipping Bennet, thought Norm. Was Mikey trying to set some kind of new world record for being incredibly annoying, or what? Because if he was, he was going about it the right way.

"If you must know, I was looking at bikes."

Mikey looked confused. "In a shop?"

"ON MY IPAD, YOU DOUGHNUT!"

"All right, all right," said Mikey. "There's no need to shout, Norm."

Straightaway Norm felt bad. It wasn't **Mikey's** fault he'd fallen asleep in class any more than it was Mikey's fault that he was just that little bit better at most things than Norm was. It was still frustrating though, having to explain. Like talking to one of his little brothers.

"Sorry, Mikey," said Norm.

"It's OK," said Mikey. "See anything you like?"

Norm thought for a moment. Had he seen anything he'd liked? Abso-flipping-lutely he had! But before he could reply, something smacked him between the eyes with such force, it felt like he'd been whacked round the head by an elephant's trunk. Not that Norm had ever actually **been** whacked round the head by an elephant's trunk before – but he imagined that's what it would feel like if he had been. It was all he could do to stay on his feet, let alone speak.

Read
MAY NEED REBOOTING
to find out what happens next!